Dead List

December Files Volume 1

Jesse Sprague

Contents

Title Page

Copyright

The Dead List   1

Too Much to Ask   6

Dead List Interlude   9

Playing Santa   11

Dead List Interlude 2   20

Red Shoes   22

Dead List Interlude 3   31

The Previous Tenant   33

Dead List Finale   43

Join Jesse's Mailing List   47

The Best Gift...   49

Books By this author   51

The Dead List

S ome nights were two-drink nights. Dr. Harris decided this was one.

He locked the door to his practice's front office. The reception desk stood empty, and he passed it without a glance and headed into his private office. He had one last virtual appointment for the night before he could go home, fend off the wife and kids, and down his stiff drinks. He'd need *at least* two drinks, given the patient.

In truth, he hoped that Fiona was a no-show.

Walking through the large, white-walled office toward his filing cabinet, Dr. Harris felt a sudden chill. He glanced around the space, decorated by plaques of his accomplishment, awards for his articles in psychiatric journals, and a few impersonal knickknacks, including a small white Christmas tree with blue glass bulbs and silver tinsel. The thermostat on the wall glowed at sixty-two degrees. It was definitely cold. The window appeared closed, but he went to double-check.

Open just a crack. One of his patients must have snuck it open. Mr. Boyle had confinement issues and was the likely culprit. Dr. Harris shoved the window shut and closed the blinds against the light fall of snow outside.

He retrieved Fiona Lester's file from the cabinet and took it back to his desk. His receptionist had left a UPS package dead center in front of his laptop, and Dr. Harris pushed it aside without looking. Instead, he opened Fiona's file. A small picture of the unassuming blonde was paper-clipped in the corner.

Most patient information was kept digitally and only accessed physically when needed, but he liked to touch Fiona's information. There was nostalgia to this patient file.

She was, after all, Dr. Harris's first high-profile client—the case that had made his name five years before. And if he was lucky and all went well with his current projects, she'd be the case that solidified his place among even higher intellectual circles.

The photo paper-clipped inside showed Fiona when she'd first come to Dr. Harris as a seventeen-year-old girl accused of killing her father. Even back then, she'd never seemed afraid—or at least not afraid of psychiatrists or the courts. But Fiona had been disturbed by something, and Dr. Harris suspected whatever that something was, it came from deep within her psyche. She'd gotten off on a self-defense plea—in no small part due to Dr. Harris. But he'd never fully believed the plea. Sure, her parents had been abusive, but there was something dark and empty behind Fiona's soft, brown eyes.

But that side of his opinion wasn't scientific. He'd testified on what he could judge based on facts.

After his latest paper published on her case, he'd realized he would never rise further in his field by talking about Fiona's past. He needed new material from her… so when she'd suggested meeting the day before Christmas, he'd agreed.

She'd signed a release early on for Dr. Harris to use her case in his research papers and books. Technically that consent was still valid, as she'd never revoked it, but he doubted Fiona had any idea he was still using her as a case study.

Fiona Lester was the most chilling example of antisocial personality disorder he'd ever seen. And no matter what the physical evidence suggested, he believed she'd played a key role in causing three deaths, not just her father's. But no new developments in her life or treatment meant no new articles to impress his colleagues. That's why he needed something monumental to happen to provide him with new material to write. His work was limited to scholarly journals, which she would never read. But if she ever did see his publications, she was certain to leave him. No way she'd accept the things he was saying about her—true though they might be.

His finger tapped on the dates he'd highlighted in his file: her father's death on Christmas Eve. Her mother's suicide one year later on Christmas morning. Then, three years down the line, the mugging that killed young Fiona's fiancée, a sweet girl named Ava, just before midnight on December 23rd. And there was poor, poor Fiona at the center of it all, always splattered in blood that was not her own.

Dr. Harris settled into his chair and opened the laptop, wishing he already had a drink. Maybe a nice, spiked eggnog.

The alert telling him that Fiona had checked in for their tele-meeting popped up five minutes early, and he stared at his screen for six minutes before opening the meeting.

The view of Fiona was skewed, tilted downward and to the side. Front and center were the blurred soles of her shoes and her long legs, covered in white hose, stretched out to rest on the computer desk. Further back from the camera, her torso leaned away into her chair. But her face, covered in a white hospital-grade mask, was only partially on the screen and blurred at the distance. He saw no point to wearing a mask during a virtual meeting, but clients often did stranger things. Red curls rioted around her head. Not natural red but a bright cherry color to match her slutty Santa outfit. Her hands, resting on her upper stomach, were covered in white fur-rimmed gloves and seemed deliberately positioned to call attention to her revealed cleavage.

Dr. Harris's eyes lingered on those breasts. Fiona had been hiding a lot under her usual sweaters. He'd never intentionally pictured her naked, but when he had on occasion visualized it, he'd imagined her chest smaller.

"Good evening, doc," Fiona said in her throaty voice. Her larynx had been damaged in childhood when her father strangled her, but the resulting sound was sexy.

"Good evening, Ms. Lester. Could you adjust your camera? It's hard for me to see you."

"No," Fiona said.

Dr. Harris considered pressing the issue, then let it go; the tone of her voice seemed serious. An odd camera angle was a small concession.

"Thank you for meeting with me last-minute," she said, remaining perfectly still, like a predator getting ready to spring.

He jotted that down in his notes.

"It's the time of year," she said. "You get that, doc? Right? The deep dark of winter is yawning open, waiting for us all to fall into it."

Dr. Harris shivered, eyes briefly leaving her perfect cleavage to her masked face. He wished he could see her expression. "But you've been doing so well. How is your new girlfriend?" He glanced down at his notes for the name. "March and you were talking about moving in together last we spoke. Having someone with you for the holidays can help if you let it."

"Oh?" Fiona's tone turned dismissive. "My girlfriend... I think she left me. No, not *think*. March *did* leave."

"Did something happen?" Dr. Harris asked, his voice cracking.

"Yeah."

No more, just that. He knew better than to ask closed questions, but Fiona's voice had him skittish. Her breasts looked great in the revealing get-up, and his eyes kept getting sidetracked from her face, but an internal voice told him that Fiona never dressed that way. He tried to focus fully on her eyes, but they were shadowed by the drooping Santa hat.

"So, Fiona, tell me what's bothering you."

"When I was little, my mom always told me that Santa had three lists."

Two. Dr. Harris corrected himself mentally.

"The Naughty List, the Nice List, and his Dead List."

Dr. Harris resisted a sigh. Every year for the five years since he met Fiona, she'd told him stories about these lists.

"Every Christmas Eve," Fiona said. "Mom would taunt me that I should be thankful to get on the Naughty List, that getting coal or no presents was certainly better than the alternative. And the alternative wasn't the Nice List, hear me? But as I got older, I started thinking that I wasn't the one who'd end up on the Dead List. Have you ever heard of the Dead List, doc?"

"Only from you, Fiona."

"Let me educate you a bit. Look beside you on the desk. There is a package and inside are some files. I call them the December Files... You see, once you leave Santa's Dead List, that's where you go."

Dr. Harris looked down at his desk. He'd shoved the package aside earlier, but now he saw it. He pulled the UPS delivery to him and opened it. Inside, as promised, were several thick manila folders with a sticky note on front that read: The December Files.

"What is this?" Dr. Harris asked. His secretary should have known better than to bring in something from a patient without alerting him. He was going to need to fire her now. "How did you —"

"Read them now, doc. Open one and see."

Dr. Harris didn't want to read anything while Fiona watched him. A voice inside him told him to hang up the call and go home to his tiresome wife and spoiled kids and his precious stiff drinks. But Fiona was his meal ticket, and her breaking down would only be good for him in the long run. So he pulled the first file off the stack and opened it to find another sticky note. This one read: Too Much to Ask.

Too Much to Ask

H olly always took one day off a year. And it was always the same day: Christmas. But in all of her years of working, she rarely received the entire day free.

This year, Holly had high hopes. It was midday on Christmas and her boss hadn't called her in yet.

Her wreaths were hung, presents wrapped, and her Christmas tree decorated. She'd taken special care with the cherub angel that she'd found at a garage sale, which glittered atop everything. A tray of cookies waited in the kitchen along with some spiced potatoes and a ham in the oven. Some cinnamon incense burned in a holder by her favorite chair and a jaunty Christmas tune played over her speakers. All that was left was to pick the first movie to binge.

Holly loved Christmas. She liked to tell everyone at work that even her name was Christmasy! But this wasn't a day for work.

Holly snuggled into her favorite chair—a lumpy recliner in faded brown—and picked up her TV remote. She thumbed through some streaming selections, trying to find the perfect Christmas movie. She enjoyed them most with a dash of romance and a bright musical score.

Before she'd settled on a flick, her phone rang.

Work.

She sighed but answered.

"Holly? Sorry to do this, but Jayson can't make it in today and the workload is nasty—"

"It's my day off!" Holly snapped, but she'd already pressed the power button on the remote to turn the television off. It helped her pride a little that, of all her co-workers, Jayson never refused to fill in for the others. Though typically he worked in-office rather than in the field, this time of year everyone did everything if needed.

"I'm afraid there is no choice. Put on that little black dress and get to it."

Holly looked down at her Christmas sweater—Rudolph's nose glowed red. She heaved another sigh. "Okay."

"You're a lifesaver."

"Hardly," Holly grumbled.

She took one last look at her festive home and then went to change.

The "little black dress"—as her boss jokingly called it—was indeed black, but it wasn't little or a dress. The robe enveloped her, and the black hood hung down over her face, obscuring her features. Holly put on sensible shoes and then grabbed her scythe.

She checked her e-mail for special instructions. Usually, her boss sent out the list of collections, but when the holidays came around, there was also a separate list of stops from St. Nick. Santa was easy to work with, but he was exacting.

First, she went to the hospital. She reaped a few babies, whose weeping families cursed fate. Then she traveled down the hall to pick up an elderly man who thanked her very kindly. She stopped by the burn ward but decided to come back in a few hours. That one wasn't ready to go yet.

Next, she took a stop from Santa's list. She picked up a man from a park; he kept asking if he could contact his wife and explain. Holly wasn't sure if he wanted to explain the knife wounds or why he'd been alone in the woods with another woman.

After that, Holly traveled to an isolated house and gathered up three college-age girls and a young man. Barely children! And each so confused. Another soul waited in the house, but he wasn't the type that Holly could help—he'd already decided not to go when his reaper came for him. The young people took some time for Holly to sort out after their traumatic experience with the thing lurking in the house. Holly tried to be patient, but she had places to go.

And none of them were home. She checked Santa's list again.

After leaving them, she took in a deep sigh and thought of the ham drying out in her oven.

But Death never takes a day off, not even for Christmas.

Dead List Interlude

Dr. Harris slapped shut the manila folder containing "Too Much to Ask." This had to be some sort of prank. What he'd just read clearly wasn't a patient file; it was probable that Fiona had written the twisted tale herself. He was honestly surprised Fiona hadn't set the story up so that "Death" directly mentioned the Dead List. He resisted an urge to violently shove all the folders off of his desk to the floor.

Instead, he forced his attention back to his computer screen and his scantily clad patient. "That's enough, Fiona. There is no purpose to me reading about make-believe figures."

"Like Santa Claus, you mean? Surely you believe in Santa."

"Like Death." Dr. Harris tried to reel in his annoyance and when he spoke again, he was pleased with the measured tone. "We are here to talk about you. I'm concerned with why you brought these here and what is going on in your life."

"Those files *are* about me, doc," Fiona said. Her throaty voice stayed low, and he thought he heard the extra roughness that often followed tears. But Fiona wasn't the sort to cry. He'd seen her angry, indignant, even cold and distant, but he'd never witnessed her cry, except in the days after Ava's death.

Dr. Harris stared hard at her. The mask covered her mouth and nose. "Can you take your mask off? I'd like to see your expression."

"No," she snapped.

"Fiona, I can only help you if you communicate with me. I can tell that something is wrong."

"No one has known me longer than you, doc. For a long time now, I've considered you almost like a friend. I assumed you knew that."

"I think fondly of you as well. But we aren't friends. I'm your psychiatrist. It's my job to help you deal with your emotions and thoughts in a productive way."

"If you want to help me, pick up the next file."

He glanced down reluctantly. The lights on his tiny Christmas tree reflected on his desk, the blue glow seeming to reach for the file. Dr. Harris grabbed it first and read the sticky note Fiona had left on the outside of the folder: Playing Santa.

Playing Santa

A half-filled cookie-sheet of cheerful Christmas shapes mocked Naomi from the flour-dusted countertop. She slammed the reindeer cookie cutter down. In the other room, gunfire sounded from a video game—one in a violent string she hadn't wanted to buy for her young son Nick. The percussive explosions punctuated the streaming Christmas music that strove unsuccessfully to convince Naomi that the holiday was going well.

Where the hell was Lee?

Lee had insisted on buying Nick the game. But her husband wasn't there, and Nick was sitting like a homicidal lump on the couch. Their two children had begged her to bake homemade cookies for Santa. But their ten-year-old, Kate, was barricaded up in her room, probably avoiding her younger brother. And six-year-old Nick had been desperate for the baking project until it meant putting down the controller.

A loud explosion cut through the brief silence.

"Fine!" Naomi spun away from the counter to stop herself from picking up the cookie-sheet and throwing it against the wall. As much as the anger in her gut pushed her to punish Nick and Kate for not helping her with the cookies, they were only kids.

They deserved their Christmas treat.

Naomi wasn't actually angry at them anyhow. Baking was simply the activity that focused the feelings welling up in her all afternoon as she waited for Lee to "Play Santa" and come home with the wrapped presents the way her dad did when she was a child.

Naomi sank into a chair at the small kitchen table. The plastic of the tabletop stuck to the sweat on her forearm. The folding chairs surrounding were the best she'd been able to do in the month since Lee had moved them all to Denver and rented this house. The neighborhood wasn't great. In fact, there'd been a murder down the street only two months before they moved in —some abused girl had killed her father and extracted his teeth. Lee said they should be thankful—drama like that just drove the rental price down on their place.

But as the chair wobbled under Naomi, she cursed each brick that backed the stove, each linoleum faux tile, and the fancy espresso maker Lee had given her as a housewarming gift to compensate her for giving up her job, her friends, her apartment, and her life.

She'd forgiven him for drinking through their savings during the six months he had been unemployed.

"And then, he doesn't bother to show up for Christmas Eve," Naomi said. She glanced at the clock, not for the first time. He should have been home from his "brief" errands by two, and it was past five.

The holiday music played on and Madonna sang about the ring she wanted from Santa. Naomi struggled not to tell the voice from the song that a damn ring never solved anything; that she was better off without it.

"Mom?" Kate popped her blonde head into the kitchen, and Naomi forced her hand out of a fist. Her fingers stretched out on the table.

"Is Daddy home yet?" Kate asked. Tempura paint smeared one cheek.

"No."

"But it's been hoooours," Kate whined.

"Bring it up with Daddy." Naomi bit back more. Of course, Naomi would get flack for Lee's absence. Wasn't that always how it worked? And as a respectful parent, trying to work in a team, she'd have to avoid blaming her husband in front of the children.

"The cookies aren't done?" Kate said. "Can I still help?"

Naomi took a measured breath. None of this was her kids' fault. Kate had probably been upstairs creating some craft present for her and Lee.

"Yes, you can help. But go clean up first." Naomi motioned to the paint splatter that dusted Kate's face like extra freckles.

Kate bobbed her head and disappeared.

Naomi followed her daughter into the kitchen doorway and watched Kate dash into the bathroom on the other side of the living room. Nick sat across the Goodwill couch the family had picked up a month before, which still reeked like it was drenched in perfume. At six, Nick barely filled one couch cushion, but the expression of concentration on his freckled face was perfectly adult.

But he wasn't an adult, neither of them were. And the Christmas tree hovering in the far corner of the room depressed Naomi. Some of their old ornaments had traveled with them, but without any presents under the tree, it looked anything but festive.

Lee had promised. He'd promised this Christmas wouldn't be a wash, not like the last one when he'd been unemployed. He'd promised to play Santa for the kids.

But now, it was Christmas Eve; the sun was touching the horizon outside the window, and no gifts, no Lee. Where the hell was he? What was he doing?

∞∞∞

Lee's arms were numb, and his shoulders ached from being stuck up above his head. The sunlight streaming from between his gloved fingertips had lost its vibrant quality. The sun must be going down.

His breaths came short, shallow, and labored. His mouth tasted like soot, and the tiny black grains had solidified on his nose, forming a frozen crust. The metal wall in front of him shoved relentlessly at his chest, which made taking in a full breath impossible. The shaft of the chimney was tighter than he'd imagined, tighter than it had looked from the roof.

Trapped.

Lee tried to shove down the mounting panic as a rasping cough made his body slip a few millimeters lower, lower and tighter. Naomi would get him help. He needed to stay calm and not make anything worse. They'd talked about this. Naomi knew where he was, and when Lee didn't show, she'd come looking.

Why hadn't she come looking already? His fingers flexed; the leather had no purchase and glided down. Just an inch up, anything. One real full breath of clean air, that's all he needed, and he could wait.

Don't scream, he warned himself as the panic built. He'd tried that, but all it did was fill his lungs further with the black air.

He needed to wait.

∞∞∞

Naomi opened the oven, and Kate slipped the full sheet of cookies into the heat. A puff of the hot air hit Naomi in the face as she shut the door.

"Can I have one when they come out?" Kate asked. A tiny blob of dough dotted her chin. The girl could get dirty in a sterile room; Naomi would swear to it.

"One. And one for your brother. We'll frost the rest. Go sit with Nick until the timer goes off, okay?"

Kate glanced over at the single place-setting remaining on the table. They'd planned an early dinner to free up the kitchen for her to bake cookies. She'd served it right on time at four-thirty. The clock said her husband was almost an hour late. Gray congealed potatoes and meat that required refrigeration stood as a testament to Lee's absence.

Where was he? Naomi wiped her forehead and watched Kate dash out of the kitchen.

Naomi crashed down into one of the chintzy chairs, too tired to be thankful the cheap legs didn't break. Lee and she had been planning how to celebrate the holiday for weeks. No way had Lee forgotten. Even if Christmas wasn't plastered on every billboard and street corner, they'd talked about it that very morning.

She'd been digging in the fridge for some cookie dough, the kind that comes in prepackaged tubes.

"No cookies." Naomi had slammed the fridge door shut.

"Doesn't Santa always get cookies?" Lee had said, taking a bite out of an energy bar.

"In this house, Santa gets cookies after he does his job." And only if she found the package.

Lee had said something, but Naomi missed it as she wondered if there was still time to make the treats from scratch. Good rolled cookies usually required the dough to be chilled overnight or, at the least, a few hours. She'd have to hurry to get the dough chilled in time to bake that evening.

"Maybe we'll leave out carrot sticks for Santa this year," Naomi said, though she didn't mean it. "My mom did that—"

"For the reindeer," Lee finished before taking another bite of his chocolatey bar. "Are you trying to tell me something?"

Lee had patted his stomach, which did have a little extra pouch this year. Any weight showed on Lee, who stood five-four and wiry. More of an elf than a Santa, really.

What had Naomi said in response? She couldn't remember.

Naomi leaned against her elbows on the plastic tabletop and waited for the memory to fade. Worrying about the past did nothing. It was immutable. No going back.

Naomi dug her cell out of her purse and dialed Lee. The tone sounded out in the living room, distinguishable under Burl Ives's dulcet tones singing "Holly Jolly Christmas." Great. Lee had left his phone behind. She hung up, slamming her phone harder than intended on the tabletop.

This might be the end of their marriage. After the move and all she'd given up, after all these years, Naomi didn't know if she could push past another missed Christmas.

No point sitting in the kitchen and stewing about it. She stood and joined the kids in the living room. On the screen, a spray of blood splattered as a zombie's head exploded. The wall behind the fallen zombie was covered with blood and a spray-painted message "The End is Nigh."

A bit highbrow for a zombie shooter game, but appropriate for the state Naomi feared her marriage was in.

Then again, what if Lee were in trouble? Stranded somewhere? Snow piled up outside the windows, suggesting various scenarios that could have delayed him. Without his phone, he'd never be able to contact her. She didn't know his number by heart; what was the chance he knew hers? Was it wrong to hope for some mishap, rather than him simply casting his family aside for some temporary distraction?

"Momma?" Nick asked.

When Naomi glanced over; Kate was the one holding the controller. This apparently meant that Nick now thought his mother was worthy of attention.

"Yeah, sweetie?" Naomi twisted the wedding ring on her finger.

"Can we light a fire?" Her son pointed to the fireplace—an ancient brick construction that was impossible to insulate. No one ever wanted to sit near it because the cold air streamed in constantly, so all the furniture was snuggled on the opposite side of the room. Still, the chimney was exciting to a city kid who'd never lived in a home with a wood-burning fireplace before.

"No, sorry sweetie. Daddy asked us not to." Naomi said, ruffling his hair.

"Why?"

Naomi shrugged. She hadn't asked. There were so many things that needed fixing in this old house; she'd just assumed anything and everything wasn't working.

"But Moooom," Nick whined.

"No, Nick." The timer beeped in the kitchen. Time to pull the cookies out and cool them. "You wanna help me put red-hots on the reindeer?"

"Yeah!" Nick sprang up from the couch and into the kitchen.

Naomi smiled. Something was wrong. Deep down, her mind fumbled for an answer that seemed just out of reach. It was like having a word on the tip of her tongue. Yet this nagging feeling was stronger—not a mild annoyance, but a desperation building inside her. She'd just have to wait for Lee to get back.

∞ ∞ ∞

Dots spun in front of Lee's eyes. He couldn't breathe, and between the pain and the knowledge he was slowly suffocating, his brain fumbled to fasten on anything else. Anything but the awareness that he was going to suffocate or freeze in this damn space.

He couldn't feel his fingers. And consciousness swam around him. If he passed out, what would happen?

His phone rang in his pocket, vibrating against his leg. Tears burst from his eyes. Naomi would hear that. She had to.

The phone silenced after only three rings, leaving him alone with his thoughts and the grime.

The walls of his tomb closed around him. Too tight. He couldn't take it. He kicked and tried to scream. Soot rushed into his mouth and only a deep rasping cough came out. His breaths picked up in pace, stirring the burn in his lungs until it screamed into his mind.

"Naomi! Help!" he shouted, though barely a croak emitted from his throat, the noise vibrating around his head, surrounding him with his own panic. Arms thrashed above his head, but due to the cramped quarters and his leather-padded fingers, his effort failed to make any sizable sound. Lee screamed soundlessly until only a desperate gasp remained.

He didn't want to die like this. Alone. Trapped.

His blackened gloves clawed at the thread of light above him.

Why wasn't she coming? She knew where he was. They'd talked about it. He was going to play Santa. She'd even warned him in the morning he was getting too fat.

So why wasn't she coming?

The day they'd rented the house and the leasing agent blithered on about the chimney, he'd leaned over to her.

"My dad used to come down on Christmas."

Naomi had laughed.

"He called it playing Santa," Lee had said, but Naomi's attention had already strayed to something else.

But she had heard him.

Did Naomi hate him so much now that she was leaving him to die?

Red eyes stared out of an otherwise innocent reindeer face. Naomi set aside the cookie and looked at the mess of Nick's decorations. Donner and Blitzen sported eight eyes, some of them not even bothering to be on the reindeer's faces.

"I wanna ice the snowflakes now," Nick said.

Naomi sighed. Hopefully, Lee's absence was just another bit of bad luck. Maybe Lee had accepted an offer for drinks with some colleagues... It wasn't like he could tell her without his phone. Of course, going out for cocktails would be almost worse than forgetting. He'd sworn he wouldn't get started drinking again. If she had to make this Christmas fun without him, she would damn well do it.

"Let's go light that fire," Naomi said. If something went wrong, she could always put the fire out. But goddamnit, this was supposed to be a fun night.

"Really, Momma?" Nick's smile made everything worth it.

"Yes. Go. Set up the starter log." Naomi strode over to the doorway after Nick and popped her head into the living room. "Kate, make sure you open the fireplace vent for your brother."

Naomi retreated into the kitchen and switched off the music. Then she pulled out a rum bottle from the freezer. She checked her latest line, drawn across the label, but nothing was missing from the bottle. That was at least something. Naomi poured a Coke into a glass of ice and added a splash of rum.

Could this Christmas get any worse?

She walked out to where the kids knelt by the fireplace. Naomi lit the starter log and crossed the room to sip her drink.

Lost in thought, she drained the drink until only ice remained, wondering what things were like back home, and if their car had finally crapped out on Lee, leaving him stranded with the presents he'd promised to buy. That was his one job: play Santa for the kids and get the gifts here. She rubbed at her nose.

Should she call the hospitals? Would that be crazy? What if she didn't, and he was hurt somewhere?

Her nose stung. Smoke.

Odd. Smelled like rubber.

Black smoke gushed out of the chimney, rolling in dark waves into the house. Naomi started forward. "Did you open the vent? That's too much smoke."

Kate pouted her lips. "I opened it."

Something must be blocking the shaft.

The smell was awful. Rubber and...

Naomi dropped her glass. Ice and glass shards skittered over the floor.

Lee was playing Santa.

Dead List Interlude 2

"Playing Santa" was an amusing story but led Dr. Harris no closer to understanding his patient's current mental state. Trying to breathe past his annoyance, Dr. Harris left the file open, his fingers splayed over the page. He couldn't afford to piss Fiona off this Christmas; his future hung on her behaving as she should.

"Well, doc? What do you think?" she said, soft. She'd been speaking quietly.

"That story seemed to miss the point. What had Lee done to be on the Dead List? Someone died on Christmas; that is tragic, but it does happen."

"Maybe," Fiona stretched the word out. "Maybe, Santa really hates frauds… those who pretend to be something they aren't." Fiona laughed. "Who says we know what Lee's sin was? It isn't in the file, but that doesn't mean he didn't deserve death. Some people are great at hiding their evil."

Like Fiona. She'd killed *at least* two times, and Dr Harris thought the number was more likely three. Yet she was free and walking the street. "That is true, Fiona. But we should talk about you, not these files. You are avoiding something."

"Aren't we all? I received the present you sent me."

"Good." He hoped she wouldn't find the box of chocolates he'd sent too personal. He didn't normally send patients gifts, for the most part. It crossed professional boundaries. Sometimes, though, he had to make exceptions. But there weren't many semi-appropriate options for him to give her this Christmas, and Fiona didn't drink alcohol. Though she had gone through a phase of harder drugs after Ava was mugged and killed.

Dr. Harris had hoped that after Ava's murder, Fiona would get caught. The blood splatter was inconclusive in the end, neither exonerating Fiona from the crime nor disproving her eyewitness statements. She claimed the attacker was a mugger who simply happened to brutally murder one woman while leaving the other untouched.

And now, Fiona was dating a new girl. He could only hope for the best.

"March got me a Christmas sweater..." Fiona's voice drifted off. "At least she got to see it on me before she left."

Perfect. Now the conversation was getting back on track. "Tell me what happened Fiona; it's clearly bothering you."

"Her leaving *is* bothering me, and I'll get to it. But first. Read the next file."

"No, this has gone too far."

"Not nearly far enough. Read it or I hang up... We're friends, right, doc? That's why you sent me a gift. As a friend, I'm asking you to do this for me."

Dr. Harris clenched his jaw before glancing nervously at the screen. He shouldn't be so open with his annoyance. And yet, Fiona didn't appear to have reacted at all.

"Humor me," Fiona said.

How much longer did he need to humor this insane woman? Yet, if he wanted to remain in her good graces, he'd need to do as she asked. Dr. Harris cracked the next file open to find a picture of two people, an immensely attractive woman and a black man in a suit. The sticky note on this one read: Red Shoes.

Red Shoes

The shoes emerge from the murky depth of my closet every winter, especially for Christmas. The rest of the year, I keep them in a box buried under my old college sweatshirts. They are perfect shoes. Red patent leather, shiny but flat—perfect for running. I tried stilettos when I was in my early twenties, but found they were too flashy. At twenty-nine, I've learned that there is an art to drawing in the right man.

Too many people nowadays are lazy. They go the easy route to seduction—show skin, everything garish and unmistakable like a neon sign around their necks saying, "Screw me." Not my style. I've always believed that you've got to put the work in.

The other morning, my boyfriend, Winston, saw me pulling the shoes out. The lid was off the box, and I ran my finger over the smooth blood-red surface of the leather.

"Those are nice, Starla," he said, leaning his shoulder against the wall by the closet. He was half-dressed for the day in dark jeans. As he spoke, he began buttoning his work shirt. His bare foot nudged mine, and he smiled. "Shall I take you out? Give you a chance to enjoy them? I could get us a reservation for tomorrow after work—go out for Christmas Eve."

"Don't bother. I'll have a chance to wear them at work." I shut the shoe box and wondered if I could distract him from my shoes by calling attention to the fact he wasn't dressed yet. I decided against it… I don't like using tricks on Winston.

He's a good guy. The type of guy who can keep a woman happy her whole life. One could say that tricks like distracting him with sex are more of treats, and I don't mind giving him treats—he's earned them. But they have to be real treats, and a distraction is not honest affection. I won't cut corners with him.

Luckily, he had to rush off to work, and the conversation didn't go any further.

Winston had almost seen the shoes on one other occasion —the day I first met him, last winter. I was coming back to my car from my favorite spot at the lake. I had the shoes in my bag, having changed into sneakers.

"A bit cold for a walk in the woods," he said. The winter wind blew his hair over his ears and across his eyes. He was standing right next to the forest path, as if waiting for someone.

People came there sometimes to pick out Christmas trees, so I wasn't too surprised to see someone, though it made me nervous.

"It's even colder for a swim," I said, smiling and touching my curls, which were turning to icicles. "I'm Starla."

But he didn't introduce himself, not then. He took off his jacket and wrapped it around me. Then offered to buy me some coffee to help me warm up. Winston is gorgeous, but that has never been the appeal to me. I've met more than my share of attractive men who are rotten on the inside. But no matter how hard I look, I can't find that side of Winston.

He's the only man I've ever considered retiring the shoes for.

I want to be good for him. Maybe next year I'll don some reindeer antlers and forget about my red shoes.

But Winston is out tonight. Christmas Eve—as it turns out he would have had to skip those reservations. He's working a double shift to cover for a co-worker whose husband just had an accident. The first time he told me was volunteering to fill in for a coworker, I followed him to see what he was really up to. Spent an awkward night in a cold car, eating salted nuts with my red shoes beside me in a box.

They never came out to play.

Every time I've followed him or suspected him of lying... he was always up to exactly what he said he was.

But he's not at my house now. I glance at the wall clock. It's just past four, and it gets dark early this late in December, so I usually set up my meetings for five o'clock. Time to get moving.

I slip the shoes on. They fit perfectly over my gray wool leggings.

Once they are on, I twist off my wedding ring… not that I've ever been married. But I like the tan line. You'd think something like a tan line would be too subtle, but it isn't. The men I want to notice always do. And the ones I don't want cluttering my view avoid me if they notice.

I picked the habit up from a waitress. Winston doesn't mind the ring, though he keeps threatening to buy me a nicer one… a real one. I wonder if I would say yes. Then, I'd have to junk my perfect winter shoes.

I shrug on my wool coat and check my makeup in the hallway mirror. Perfect.

On my way out the door, I dig into my key bowl. The keys have sunken into the yellow-white stones filling the ceramic container. I shake a few free. They clink together.

As I step outside I note that many of the neighbors have their Christmas lights on, even though it isn't dark quite yet. Mine are lit too. Winston put them up, and he'll take them down, too. I've never been big on Christmas.

Santa bugs me. Always has. Not that I don't like the idea of rewarding good little boys and girls. But I feel that coal isn't teaching the others much of a lesson (nor do I think the old guy gives out nearly enough coal. Some of those *good* little ones are shits.) Still, my bigger issue is that the whole St. Nick thing skips the majority of humanity—adults. And many of them never learned how to be good.

St. Nick doesn't put in the work. He's lazy.

Christmas isn't the only winter holiday I have these issues with. I mean come on! New Year's? As if we could erase the fetid, rotting deeds from our souls and come out clean. Worse is that people actually make resolutions, to help purge their consciences, and then are too lazy to keep them.

And don't get me started on Valentine's Day. Really? A day to celebrate love? Because none of us can be bothered to remember to do something romantic on any other day of the year. It's lazy. That's all it is. So, for thirteen years now, I've had my own way of celebrating the winter holidays.

My red shoes clack on the sidewalk. I hop into my car and start driving.

This isn't the first time I've broken out my shoes this year. So, rather than heading to a bar, which is the perfect first outing, I pull in across from a park on the edge of a large greenstrip. The lot is nearly empty due to the time and the date but the shops across the street are still lit. I have a meeting lined up, but it's only half past four. That gives me a little time to spare before the guy's set to arrive. There's a hotdog vendor on the sidewalk, his breath steaming in the cold.

Sounds tasty.

The grassy expanse of the park is sparsely populated. A few kids are on the playset with over-bundled parents watching them. Teenagers lounge at the edge of the woods on the grass borders. I take careful note of their location before heading over to the vendor and ordering my Christmas Eve dinner.

A man is staring at me from a bench, and when I catch his gaze, he winks. I didn't expect to get noticed here. But since my scheduled meeting isn't for another half an hour, I figure I have time to kill. I head over with my hot dog and smile.

"You mind if I sit here?" I ask, brushing my hair behind my ear.

He nods, but rather than meeting my eyes, he's looking at my legs. Schmuck. I sit beside him and cross my legs, letting one patent leather shoe dangle from my foot. His hands are gloved, so I can't tell if he's wearing a ring or not.

"Cold day for the park," he says.

I'd bet he considered asking me if I was here on a date.

"You here with your kids?" I ask, taking a big bite of the hot dog. I could be dainty, but that's too obvious. The problem with men is that most of them, even the generally good ones, will take the bait if you make it obvious enough. Offer to blow a guy in the park and you'll get a line of them. But I don't want the ones who are temptable... I want the ones who will go out of their way to find corruption. The ones whose souls leak tar, polluting the world around them.

He's said something. I didn't catch it.

"You meeting someone here?" he asks, glancing at the playground, though I doubt he gives a damn if I have a husband or a kid about to show up. Men only care about details like that if they are seeking a genuine connection.

Winston would have cared. A bite of guilt hits me, thinking about him.

"I'm meeting an old friend in about fifteen." I shrug. Then I glance back at the hotdog vendor. "I should've thought to get a coffee."

"Tell you what, if you give me your number, I'll go over there and get you whatever you like." He nods at a real coffee shop across the way.

I giggle. I'm good at giggling. We both pull out our cells, and I give him my number. Then he heads over to the coffee place to get me a double dirty chai.

No proof yet that he's awful. But I can find a lot on a guy through his phone number. I fiddle with my phone as I wait. I find his full name. Nathan Redbirch. Married with a teenage daughter.

I bet his kids are nasty, and I bet they never get coal. I blame Santa. Maybe if Nathan had gotten something more persuasive than coal as a child, he wouldn't be who he is today. I'll make damn sure his kids understand what happens if you're naughty.

Nathan comes back with my drink, and I sit there chatting with him for another five minutes. I try not to think about Winston, but he keeps sneaking into my thoughts. I never heard him get the call to go to work. But I have no reason to distrust him... nothing except this feeling I've had since he saw the shoes. A feeling like he's watching me.

"I really do have to go meet my friend." I smile and stand. Though Tony isn't a friend. I don't mind fibbing to this jerk.

"I'll call you," Nathan says.

"I look forward to it." He's earned a second meeting with the red shoes. I'll bet this jerk gets his wife flowers every Valentine's Day, on her birthday too. I bet he thinks that's good enough.

As I walk across the park, my phone beeps.

'I'm here. Where are you?' the text says. I appreciate that it is grammatically sound and written out. I can't stand people who abbreviate in texts. I put a lot of effort into these meetings, and I expect a little effort in return.

I text back, *'Meet me by the North Path. There's a nice spot back in the woods.'*

I hurry across the grass towards the trees. Frost rubs off on my shoes. Kids squeal from the playset on the north side of the park. I bet their teachers give them projects to make on Valentine's Day... corrupting an already disgusting holiday. They put no effort in. None at all.

My phone buzzes. I check it in case it is my naughty boy. It isn't. The screen reads: Jayson Winston Prior. Right from the start of our relationship I called him Winston, I like the formality of full names in my phone, though I never call him by his first name. It's too trendy for me. He writes that his coworker was able to come in after all. He's getting off in an hour and wants to know if he should pick up some wine.

I text that I'd like white, and it may be closer to an hour and a half until I'm home. Then I finger the phone, considering turning around. Wouldn't my time and effort be better spent with him? As I'm thinking, the phone buzzes.

'I love you.' Winston texts back. *'It was around this time last year we met in the park. Do you still go to that lake?'*

I scrunch my forehead. Why does there seem to be a ton of judgment in that text?

I forget about him when I see Tony waiting at the entrance to the footpath. This time of year, no one takes the paths. Especially on Christmas Eve. It's too cold, especially paths like this that go down to the lake. And by lake, I mean big enough not to freeze, but too small for boats. And deep. So ridiculously deep.

Perfect for me.

"Hey, you look gorgeous, Starla" he says.

"Thanks, Tony." He's not bad himself. Styled blond hair and a body that must take at least an hour a day of weights to maintain. He puts a lot of effort into his looks, more than is right. I mean, I believe in dedication, but one has to choose the right thing to be dedicated to.

Like loyalty and love.

I lead him onto the path, and once we are out of sight, he kisses me. His tongue invades my mouth. I let him take a brief grab at my body before pulling away.

"I have something special for you tonight," I say, smiling. My wool coat has fallen open and lets the freezing air in.

It's a fifteen-minute walk down to the lake, and Tony follows me without reservations. The pictures I texted him the night before help with that. Though I wish he'd stop touching me.

I shiver as his hand slides over my butt.

"We could always get a hotel," he says as we walk.

"No matter how many times you make that suggestion, I'm going to say no."

"It's fucking freezing."

Swearing. Ugh. I don't keep a swearing jar. But I'll take his tongue. I always take the teeth. If you polish teeth up, round them off like little stones, they look like ivory. I've filled a decorative bowl with them back at my house, where I keep my keys. Some days, especially in the summer, I like to run my fingers through and think of how much better the world is with those teeth in my bowl.

As we reach to shore of the lake, I slip my hand into my pocket and wrap my fingers around my daddy's pocketknife. His teeth are in my bowl too, but I like the knife better. It's the knife that taught me right from wrong.

I turn to Tony and grin.

"You've been a very naughty boy," I say.

∞ ∞ ∞

I wash the blood off my hands in the lake and stare down at my reflection.

Click.

The sound comes from behind me, and I spin around. Winston stands there in the shadows, frowning.

"What the hell!" I say. Then I notice the cold metal in his hands. A gun. How lazy. Probably better I don't complain about the lack of effort when it's pointed at me.

He says nothing but tosses a small box on the ground in front of me. A ring box.

"What are you doing?" I ask.

"Hush, love," he says. "I've been trying… so much. But every year, you just keep coming here."

"It's not what…"

"It's exactly what I think. I've known who you are from the day we met. I'd hoped you'd let it go. I see now that was stupid of me. Pick the box up."

I don't have to, but I do. I know what's in it. I crack it open to find an engagement ring.

"You have a choice," he says. "The way I see it there are three ways this goes. You kill me, I kill you or you put that ring on and—"

I raise my hand to stop him. No need for him to finish. I know exactly what he means. I'd have to stop with the shoes if we got married. Being in a relationship is one thing, but the ring, that's the promise. He knows me well enough, especially if he knows enough about my lake habits to know I'd never have an affair. So if I marry him, he knows I'll stop.

I could try to trick him.

But I don't want to.

I take the shoes off my feet, letting my toes dig into the rocky shore as I turn and throw them out onto the placid surface of the lake. They splash and are gone.

I guess I'm getting married. Someone else will have to keep up with St. Nick's dirty work.

Dead List Interlude 3

What the hell was that story? Dr. Harris wondered. Fiona's December Files were only getting nastier.

Dr. Harris sighed and closed the file for "Red Shoes." There were several more folders on the stack, and he had a distinct feeling that he didn't want to read any of them. He stared at Fiona's masked face on his computer screen. He realized he hadn't seen her move all night. And the jaw was wrong. Now that he looked closely, Fiona's was pointier, longer. This face was shorter and round. That was not Fiona. That changed things.

Who the hell was on the screen? A darker consideration filtered in—was the person even alive? The lack of movement seemed to point to a negative answer to that question.

He needed to get off the call and get out... probably call the police. Still, he spoke to whoever was on the screen. "And how does this last narrative belong in the December Files? I assume you are implying that Starla was on the Die List. But she didn't die."

"The Dead List. And no, she changed her path, in time." The voice came out of the computer, but if he strained his ears, Dr. Harris thought he heard an echo. "But Starla had her own Dead List, now didn't she? Or maybe she was an agent for Santa—those that do his dirty work often don't know it. Except she didn't finish her list, did she? Nathan *Redbirch* wasn't checked off."

The way she said the name made him uncomfortable. If it hadn't been for the last name, he might have suspected the fictional character in the file was meant to be her father, Nathanial Lester. "That upsets you?"

"Names and places may have been changed, doc. Six years ago, she didn't finish her list. You think she's some sort of metaphor for me... but that's not true. I'm nothing like her."

Dr. Harris judged that he could get out the door before she knew he suspected. His heart pounded in his chest, and the still breasts on the screen took on a new meaning.

He'd been right all along about Fiona; the woman was insane, whatever label was put on her madness. He gripped the arms of his chair, ready to push himself to his feet. "Should we look at the last file?"

"We're not done with 'Red Shoes' yet. Someone saved her, doc. You were supposed to save me... Have you done that?"

Dr. Harris stood up, but before he could take a single step, the door to his private office squeaked open behind him. Dr. Harris turned to see a slender female form walk in from the front office.

He already knew.

He didn't know who was on the computer, who the dead girl was who he'd been staring at, but it definitely wasn't Fiona, because Fiona was here with him. She wore a loose-fitting Christmas sweater covered in perky Christmas trees surrounding a red skull sporting a Santa hat. Her blonde hair had been pulled back in a severe bun. She was a small woman, fragile. He could overpower her if needed.

"Don't stand up. Sit down *now*, doc," she said. "Open the next file."

"Fiona, let's talk."

"No!" Fiona yelled. She lifted her hand and displayed a revolver. She twitched the muzzle in his direction. "*Open* the next file."

Facing that muzzle, Dr. Harris thought it was a good idea to play along for the moment. The next sticky note, covered in bright red ink, read: The Previous Tenant.

The Previous Tenant

T he present appeared under Kate's tree about a week before Christmas. When she saw the red and green wrapping with tiny elves dancing over the paper, she set her purse down on the table by the front door and called out into her house.

"Momma?"

No reply. But the present must have come from somewhere and her mother was the only other person with a key to her house. At twenty-two, Kate's focus was on work. She preferred to live alone rather than invite the drama she'd watched her friends go through with their live-in partners. Even the drama of trying to pick a movie with her last horror-loving boyfriend had been too much for Kate. She'd make time for love later.

Kate slipped her keys onto the hook above her purse on the entryway table, and then carefully pulled off her shoes and placed them neatly in place on the shoe rack. There was no excuse for messiness. She headed further into the house along the walkway between the main living areas. She glanced around the small home as she walked. The open kitchen was neat, just as she'd left it: not an item out of place. The sliding glass door out to the yard showed only a vacant patch of grass. Through the door into the bathroom, she saw that it was empty, too. Unless someone was rude enough to hide in the bedroom, there was no evidence of a visitor, aside from the neatly wrapped gift.

A smile played on her lips. The small box had to be from her mother, and it was nice to know someone had thought of her, even if Kate didn't like the clutter of presents on the floor before

Christmas morning.

She headed into the kitchen and poured herself a glass of red wine. The glub-glub of it coming out and then splashing into the glass seemed unreasonably loud in the house. Kate carried the full glass and the bottle of wine and took a closer look at the present. It was small and squarish, the size to hold a ring or something of the like. She picked it up, and the box seemed too heavy for jewelry. The festive green ribbon tickled her knuckles.

There was no card or tag. Kate turned the box in her hands and then looked back under the Christmas tree at her neatly swept floor. She'd have to find another place for the present for a week until Christmas Day. For the moment, Kate deposited the box on the mantle above her cold fireplace.

As she pulled out her neatly marked storage container for pretzels and hummus from the fridge, she decided that after dinner she would call her mom and thank her for the gift. It was odd of her mom to stop by during the week. Usually, her mom was either at work or with her new husband. Odder than that, her mom had hated Christmas ever since the tragedy that killed Kate's father.

After his death, their family hadn't celebrated Christmas, but Kate had missed the festivities. She yearned the holiday in her adult life, even if she never wanted to encounter another Santa again—not after seeing her father in that red suit being pulled out of the chimney. She avoided malls with their decorative North Poles and white-bearded Santas, but otherwise, she wanted to enjoy Christmas with the rest of the world.

But Kate's mom and her little brother avoided anything Christmas-related.

All the more reason to thank her mom for the gift.

After making a quick dinner, continuously glancing at the bright package on her mantle, Kate ate and called her mom. No one answered, so Kate left a message thanking her. She tidied up after dinner and once the kitchen was back in perfect order, grabbed a book to read by the fireplace and her Christmas tree.

She'd splurged on the tree, getting a large fir that dominated the room. And then she'd handmade paper snowflakes to hang from its branches among the cheap store-bought ornaments. She'd kept everything white—the whole thing seemed neater that way, just white and green.

As she settled down to read, her eyes slid over the tree, appreciating the calculated beauty. Then her eyes caught on the present, sitting on the wood floor.

"I could swear I picked you up," she said. Kate didn't question herself. She knew she had moved it. Could she have deposited the box back under the tree without realizing and forgotten? But she didn't even like it under the tree.

Before cracking her book, Kate moved the gift back to the mantle. She enjoyed another glass of wine and her book but couldn't help glancing up all evening to check that the present hadn't moved.

She went to bed late and dreamed she was searching for the source of a rotting smell all over the house, only to discover it originated by the tree. A needle with thick thread stuck out of the present, the metallic thread trailing off into the darkness so Kate couldn't see the end of it. Glassy eyes, like the eyes of a doll or a mounted steer's head, peered out of the darkness. When she woke, promptly at 6 A.M. as usual, she decided to tuck the gift away in the coat closet with the few she'd purchased for herself.

Instead, sleep-deprived after a night of bad dreams, she fell back asleep.

After finally getting up at 8 A.M., Kate's morning was busy. Sleeping in was very unlike her, but being late to work was unthinkable. She rushed to get ready for work by 9 A.M. But as she grabbed a breakfast bar from one of her Tupperware containers, she found her eyes dragging over to the tree.

The present rested under the branches, a few stray fir needles on the wooden floor. Kate's stomach lurched. She grabbed her broom and quickly swept both the present and the tree's mess out into a dust pan.

Then she stood over the dust pan. She could just throw everything away and have done with it. But this might be the first present her mom had purchased for her since she was a child. Kate picked out the box with shaking hands and set it carefully, and purposefully, on the kitchen windowsill.

Presents didn't move by themselves and that would be proved when she got hom and it was in the *correct* spot.

Only the bright display on the clock telling her she only had twenty-five minutes to drive to work—a drive that took at least that in morning traffic—spurred Kate to turn away from the gift, dump the dustpan, and hurry out the door to her car.

She tried to think of anything else on her drive to work and made it to her desk with two minutes to spare.

After the initial round of morning meetings, Kate checked her messages. Her mom had returned her voicemail—playing tag they used to call it—and said she hadn't left a gift or even stopped by. She suggested that maybe the present came from Kate's ex.

Dwight *did* want to rekindle their fling, Kate conceded mentally. During the final fight of their short-lived relationship, he'd accused her of tanking all personal connections because she was afraid of needing anyone. He hadn't been entirely wrong. And given his obsession with all-things horror, maybe the gift was from him, and he was somehow pranking her with the box moving around—though she had no idea how he would accomplish such a thing. Still, Dwight didn't have a key to her home. Kate gave him a tentative call to ask him if he'd visited and left a surprise for her. Once again, she left a voicemail.

Kate tried to convince herself that her ex had left the gift. But her heart raced, and her nerves jangled. Something was wrong.

After work, she drove home. Standing outside the front door, she paused, trying to make herself reach out to the doorknob. When she did open the door, she held her keys in her hands, the largest sticking out between two fingers—a self-defense maneuver her mother had taught her. Kate was logically certain she was safe, but that didn't stop the crawling sensation over her skin.

Inside, the house looked the same as always, but she didn't

drop her purse on the little table by the door or hang up her keys. She had no intention of relaxing until she saw that box on the kitchen windowsill. No one was there to see her look stupid—or if they were, then her precautions weren't stupid.

Kate walked into the house. Her tree was the same, paper snow drifted over the green branches. But the present was back under the tree. Kate stared at the bright red and green wrapping. Her heart pounded so loud it seemed deafening in her ears. This wasn't some prank; she felt it in her bones.

That's when she saw him out of the corner of her eye. A man, enveloped in shadows, crouching in the corner behind the Christmas tree. A tattered Santa hat hung off his head—only recognizable in the darkness by the white trim. In one hand he held large pair of shears. In the other Kate caught the glint of a needle.

She could see right through his body to the wall.

White teeth gleamed from a too-wide smile. Kate didn't scream. She froze, mind racing, trying not to look directly at this horror, all while not being able to avert her attention. If he didn't know she'd seen, he might lurk, savoring the show. She couldn't give away that she knew he was there... whatever he was.

Don't look at him, don't look. He'll know you're looking, she thought.

She still saw more than she wanted to. His pallor had a grayish tone, and the shadows seemed to grind into his features, giving his eyes a skull-like hollow. Where his lips drew back into something vaguely akin to a smile, long teeth showed, clenched together. Little stitches marred the skin of his arm and neck, as if he'd sutured closed wounds with a dark thread.

Kate didn't care if the terrifying specter was real or imagined. She only wanted out.

Thinking back to the macabre scene of her father's death, Kate knew that confronting such terrors head on didn't help. Only by skirting around, by pretending she didn't feel or see had she gotten through that day and the weeks that followed.

Kate could do it again.

Taking in a deep breath, Kate kept her eyes aimed at the present on the floor. She pretended she hadn't seen the apparition. She smiled as if the gift delighted her. Then she casually and painfully slowly turned around and walked out of the house. She walked at a measured stroll to the car, counting the cracks in the sidewalk to keep herself from bolting. She climbed into the car and fumbled at sticking the key in the ignition.

Were the shadows by the house moving?

Kate didn't look.

She told herself that if she looked, she was either insane or dead.

The key slid into place, and she started the car, drove out onto the street, and *then* called the police.

When the police drove by her parked car, she followed them back to the house. She showed them the tree. The present was gone. The officers found no evidence of a break-in and just side-eyed each other at her story. They offered to post a patrol.

Kate said no.

Then she asked them to come with her for a moment while she packed a bag. Logical or not, she wasn't going back into that house alone, not ever.

Kate stayed with her mom for a few weeks while she broke her lease and looked for a new place—one with roommates. She hired movers to go back for most of her things and repurchased anything she had to leave behind. Dwight went in with the movers to retrieve her legal documents. Turns out, her opinion had shifted on romance. Now the only thing that scared her more than relying on someone else was being alone. She was willing to give her ex another go.

By New Year's, she wasn't sleeping alone. By the following Christmas, her nightmares had mostly faded, though she didn't allow Dwight to put up a Christmas tree and mall Santas or just men with Santa hats on the street still gave her panic attacks.

After the fact, she wondered what exactly the ghastly experience had meant. Maybe the gruesome man had been there to warn her? But that hadn't been how it felt. Still, she needed to know.

She did some research on the house she'd left. She found an article detailing a disappearance from that house several years back, on Christmas Day. The owner had planned to propose to his girlfriend, but she went missing. Shortly thereafter, so did he. Eventually, the woman's body showed up—or parts of it. She'd been stuffed, her skin sewed together with heavy thread and glass eyes fitted into her skull. The man was never found. A little further digging revealed that the man had been a hobby taxidermist.

Kate didn't need to know any more than that.

Another year passed, and she never went back. She and Dwight found a bigger apartment in an upscale neighborhood with a state-of-the-art security system. Life stayed normal—just how Kate wanted it.

Then, around noon on Christmas Eve two years after Kate fled from the apparition, she was home alone. The universe reached out to her in the form of a pretty girl wearing a college sweatshirt. Kate's doorbell rang, and she peered through the peephole at this presumed student, looking harrowed. Kate considered not answering, but something in the terrified expression on the young woman's face moved Kate to crack the door and look out past the security chain.

"I'm Masha," the young woman said. "I was wondering if we could talk… I live in a house I think you used to live in and—"

Kate shut the door. She didn't want anything to do with the house or whatever was inside it. She'd gotten away.

"Please," Masha said through the closed door. "I found this police report you filed. Would you please just answer a few questions? Would you mind?"

Kate did mind. Whatever Masha had come to say would open wounds. But Kate feared the wounds that Masha faced might be far more real and far, far more deadly. Kate opened the door.

Masha refused the offer of tea and launched into her own all-too-familiar tale of a gift showing up and dreams of needles with thick thread. She didn't mention the spectral man, but Kate would have bet this sweet girl had seen him.

"Did you open the box?" Kate asked.

"I didn't. But Louise... that's my friend, threatened to. Now I can't find her anywhere. I'm afraid she did open it. And I need to know... I mean... we all thought we were imagining things until Lou disappeared."

"Call the police."

Masha shook her head. "She didn't disappear... hat way. Something dragged her..." Masha stopped and took a deep breath. "Something dragged her into the shadows. I watched it happen. There's no where for her to have gone but she isn't there anymore. She has to be in the house somewhere. The police don't believe us. We can't just leave her there."

"We?" Kate asked, eyes narrowing.

"Yeah. I rented the place with Louise and another girl. And my boyfriend has been staying with us. Would you tell me what you know about the house?"

Kate told Masha the little she'd discovered about the man who used to live there and his erstwhile fiancée. That was the information that Masha wanted, what she'd come to hear. But Kate ended on the point she really wanted to make. "Get out of that house. Don't go back for any reason."

Masha smiled softly and thanked Kate for the advice.

Kate watched the girl leave. Masha would go back. Of course she would.

When Dwight came home that night, Kate relayed the whole experience. To her surprise, he laughed.

"Have you started watching horror movies?" he asked.

"No," Kate said. She hated horror movies; her life seemed too close to one already.

"Well, that sounds just like this scene that's in a lot of them."

Kate gave him a look and tapped her foot.

Dwight smiled, liking this more than Kate thought he should. "Masha is the final girl in the story—the sole survivor or final victim in a horror movie massacre. *You're* the previous tenant; the one who was smart enough to get away. Are you sure she wasn't pulling your leg? Sounds like a weird prank to me."

But Kate had seen the terror in Masha's eyes. If Kate was the previous tenant, that meant that Masha was living the horror movie. And Kate didn't wish that on anyone. That night, she couldn't sleep.

Two days later, the day after Christmas, Kate's conscience got to her. She steadied herself; the truth was she'd never gotten past this nightmare. If she didn't face the terror, maybe she'd never get past this. Either Masha and her friends were in the house and in dire trouble, or Dwight was correct, and Masha's visit was a prank based on the crazy police report Kate filed years earlier.

Kate needed to know.

She went to the house and parked. Several cars lined the driveway, most rundown with fast food wrappers and used textbooks filling the backseat of some. Looked like evidence of college kids residing there. Kate went up to the house. She knocked.

The door swung open to the pressure of her knuckles, revealing a darkened interior.

"Hello?" she called. "Masha?"

No answer.

A chill ran down Kate's spine. Coming here was stupid, so stupid. The memory of the apparition's smile filled her mind along with the gleam of his needle. But if she left now, she'd never know if there really was something to fear of what was in the box.

Kate took one step inside and smelled pine. She saw the Christmas tree in the living area, half lying against the wall, ornaments spilled over the floor. A green and red wrapped box lay in the center of the floor, the wrapping ripped and the lid partway off, showing a shadowed lump inside.

Nope.

She decided she would rather never unravel the mystery than end up a bloody part of it. She could live without knowing what was in the box—because that meant she was alive.

Kate turned around and left. As far as she could tell, the difference between a previous tenant and a victim was knowing when to walk away.

Dead List Finale

T he "Previous Tenant" file stood open on Dr. Harris's desk, though he'd stopped reading it, stopped even pretending that he was reading it. He stood, half leaning over the file, Fiona's revolver pressed against his back. Instead of reading, he looked past the computer at his small white Christmas tree. There were no presents under it, but there would be plenty under the tree in his house. He had an urge to rush there and hug his children—the three monsters. Maybe even kiss his frigid wife.

Finishing the files seemed like a bad plan given the woman standing behind him. Especially given that the woman was Fiona Lester, a psychopath who had already gotten away with at least one murder in court and probably two more that never went to trial.

"Fiona, whatever point you are trying to make, I'm afraid it is beyond me."

"I've always been a Kate," Fiona said quietly, her voice coming from directly behind him. The gun barrel dug in painfully between his shoulder blades, and she wiggled it for emphasis. "I got away from my dad before he could deliver on his promise to kill me. I got out just in time when my mom started losing it. I avoided getting caught in the mess. I never killed *anyone*, but you didn't like that, did you?"

The question didn't seem like one he should answer. His mind raced, trying to find the right words to calm Fiona down.

"I've read all your articles, doc. Every last one."

Shit! Dr. Harris tried to think of something, anything to say to that. But before he could form a word, the muzzle of the gun pressed harder into his back.

Fiona whispered now, the heat and wetness of her breath against his neck. The gun moved upward until the metal brushed against the back of his head, mussing his hair. "You think I'm crazy, that I killed all of them, but I didn't. I never would. My parents deserved to die horribly. They were on the Dead List. Always were... and sometimes Santa needs a little help. No one would ever believe me that I didn't kill them because it was clear I *wanted* them dead. But Ava? March?"

March? Dr. Harris flinched at the name. Fiona had said her *girlfriend* left, but the very inclusion of her name implied worse. Had Fiona killed her or... Dr. Harris swallowed hard. The girl on the screen.

Fiona hissed, anger dripping from each word. "Ava was taken from me, and you tell everyone in your stupid articles that I murdered her. That I stabbed Ava over and over and over again."

"If I'm wrong," Dr. Harris started, "I can correct it—"

"Shut up. I'm not done talking. Truth is, I read that article, and I thought, 'Okay. I'll accept that interpretation. I know you're wrong about me.' But last night, I thought March might enjoy some chocolates while I prepared dinner. I opened your stupid Christmas gift early. Look at her, doc... Look at March. I loved her..."

He stared at the screen, at the beautiful corpse that he'd thought he was conversing with all night. Dr. Harris pondered feigning innocence, but Fiona had never been stupid. She *knew* and lying about what must have happened would only anger her more. "You shared the chocolates I sent."

Why hadn't Fiona eaten them, too? Or had she just missed the few he'd doctored? He mentally kicked himself for not considering that. All his plans were out the window!

"I did share your *gift*. She loved them, right up until she..." Fiona seemed to choke on the words. "One question for you, doc... did you know that I'd share? Did you *mean* for me to kill her first and then off myself? Or was I your sole target? Did you want to get rid of me to renew my story, give it a better ending?"

He had to think of some sort of explanation. Maybe March was allergic to peanuts? "I didn't—"

"It doesn't matter. You see, it's my ending now. For once, I get to choose. And if the whole world is going to think I'm a killer... Then I am going to be one."

Join Jesse's Mailing List

Want more?

That's not problem! There is plenty more insanity to be had.

Sign up for Jesse's mailing list at Jessesprague.com (or reader's group as she likes to call it) for updates on her latest projects and extra perks like character interviews, early release information, insights into her process, and best yet FREE exclusive short stories!

Did you miss reading her other works? Check out Bone River

The Best Gift...

Is a review.

Enjoyed the book? As an independant female author, reviews are my lifeline. They are how readers find new books and decide what is right for them. Without your help, other readers may never find me!

So go on Amazon and/or Goodreads and say what you like, what you didn't like, or anything else you feel. Even just leaving a star rating can help!

Books By this author

Aspect Wars

Bone River
Bone Yard

5Th City Chronicles

Beneath 5th City
Project Eo
Red Angel

The Drambish Contaminate Series

Spider's Kiss
Spider's Gambit
Spider's Choice

Anthologies

Love in the Wreckage
Monster's Movies & Mayhem
Once Upon Now
Undeath by Chocolate

Printed in Great Britain
by Amazon

28504309R00036